Toys

Les jouets

ley joo-*eh*

Illustrated by Clare Beaton

Illustré par Clare Beaton

BARRON'S

doll

la poupée

lah poop-*eh*

ball

le ballon

leh bal-*oh*

blocks

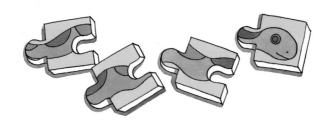

les cubes

ley k'yoob

car

la voiture

lah vwot-*yoor*

fish

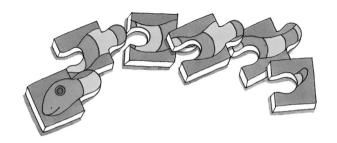

le poisson

leh pwah-*soh*

drum

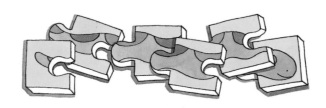

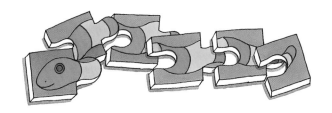

le tambour

leh tom-*boor*

teddy bear

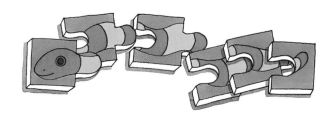

le nounours

leh noo-*noorss*

puzzle

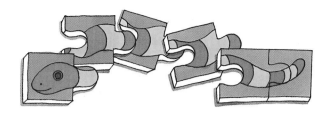

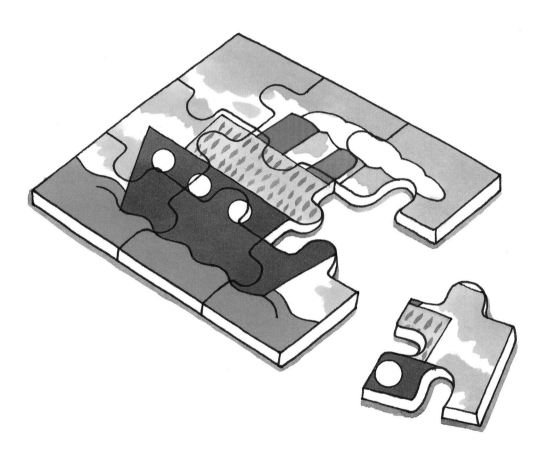

le puzzle

leh *pooz*-leh

tricycle

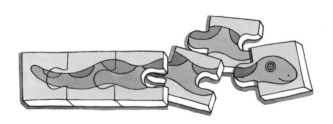

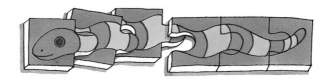

le tricycle

leh tree-*seekl'*

skates

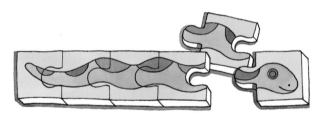

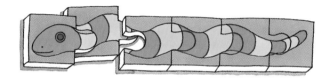

les patins

ley pat-*ah*

crayons

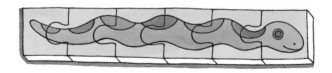

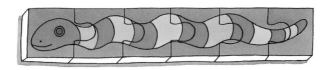

les crayons

ley cray-*oh*

A simple guide to pronouncing the French words★

- Read this guide as naturally as possible, as if it were English.
- Put stress on the letters in *italics,* e.g. lah vwot-*yoor.*
- Remember that the final consonants in French generally are silent.

les jouets	ley joo-*eh*	**toys**
la poupée	lah poop-*eh*	**doll**
le ballon	leh bal-*oh*	**ball**
les cubes	ley k'yoob	**blocks**
la voiture	lah vwot-*yoor*	**car**
le poisson	leh pwah-*soh*	**fish**
le tambour	leh tom-*boor*	**drum**
le nounours	leh noo-*noorss*	**teddy bear**
le puzzle	leh *pooz*-leh	**puzzle**
le tricycle	leh tree-*seekl'*	**tricycle**
les patins	ley pat-*ah*	**skates**
les crayons	ley cray-*oh*	**crayons**

★There are many different guides to pronunciation. Our guide attempts to balance precision with simplicity.

Text and illustrations © Copyright 2003 by B SMALL PUBLISHING, Surrey, England.
First edition for the United States, its Dependencies, Canada, and the
Philippines published in 2003 by Barron's Educational Series, Inc.
All rights reserved. No part of this book may be reproduced in any form, by photostat,
microfilm, xerography, or any other means, or incorporated into any information retrieval
system, electronic or mechanical, without the written permission of the copyright owner.
Address all inquiries to:
Barron's Educational Series, Inc., 250 Wireless Boulevard, Hauppauge, New York 11788 (http://www.barronseduc.com)
International Standard Book Number 0-7641-2612-1
Library of Congress Control Number 2003101097
Printed in Hong Kong   9 8 7 6 5 4 3 2 1